THE LIBRARY OF
FLUTE
CLASSICS

SOLO PART

WITH SPECIAL THANKS TO VANESSA GIBBONS FOR EDITORIAL ASSISTANCE

THIS BOOK COPYRIGHT © 1999 BY AMSCO PUBLICATIONS,
A DIVISION OF MUSIC SALES CORPORATION, NEW YORK, NY.

ORDER NO. AM 948882
US INTERNATIONAL STANDARD BOOK NUMBER: 0.8256.1707.3
UK INTERNATIONAL STANDARD BOOK NUMBER: 0.7119.7587.6

EXCLUSIVE DISTRIBUTORS:
MUSIC SALES CORPORATION
257 PARK AVENUE SOUTH, NEW YORK, NY 10010 USA
MUSIC SALES LIMITED
8/9 FRITH STREET, LONDON W1V 5TZ ENGLAND
MUSIC SALES PTY. LIMITED
120 ROTHSCHILD STREET, ROSEBERY, SYDNEY, NSW 2018, AUSTRALIA

PRINTED IN THE UNITED STATES OF AMERICA BY
VICKS LITHOGRAPH AND PRINTING CORPORATION

AMSCO PUBLICATIONS
NEW YORK/LONDON/PARIS/SYDNEY

CONTENTS

		Piano	Flute
Joachim Andersen	Scherzino	4	5
Johann Sebastian Bach	Minuet	5	5
	Gavotte	6	6
	Sonata No. 2	8	7
	Brandenburg Concerto No. 4	10	8
	Brandenburg Concerto No. 5	14	10
Ludwig van Beethoven	Symphony No. 4	18	12
	Symphony No. 7	18	12
	Symphony No. 9	20	13
	Serenade	21	13
	Minuet in G	22	14
Hector Berlioz	Symphonie Fantastique	24	15
Georges Bizet	Habañera	26	16
Luigi Boccherini	Concerto in D Major	28	17
Johannes Brahms	Waltz	30	18
	Symphony No. 1	32	19
	Symphony No. 4	33	19
Frédéric Chopin	Minute Waltz	34	20
	Nocturne	38	22
Claude Debussy	Prelude to the Afternoon of a Faun	41	26
	Rêverie	44	27
Antonin Dvořák	Humoresque	50	24
Friedrich von Flotow	Ah! So Pure	48	28
Christoph Willibald von Gluck	Minuet and Dance of the Blessed Spirits	62	29
Benjamin Godard	Berceuse	53	32
	Légende Pastorale	56	30
George Frideric Handel	Sonata No. 2	66	34
	Sonata No. 5	72	33

		Piano	Flute
Miska Hauser	Cradle Song	74	40
Franz Joseph Haydn	Serenade	76	36
	Trio No. 4	78	38
Felix Mendelssohn	Spring Song	82	42
	On Wings of Song	86	41
	Scherzo	88	44
Wolfgang Amadeus Mozart	Quartet in D	96	46
	Concerto No. 2	98	47
Mozart-Andersen	Cadenzas for Mozart Concerto No. 2		54
Jacques Offenbach	Barcarolle	93	59
Émile Pessard	Andalouse	118	60
Johann Joachim Quantz	Arioso	122	62
Nikolai Rimsky-Korsakov	Song of India	126	63
	Flight of the Bumblebee	129	66
	Scheherazade	138	68
Anton Rubinstein	Melody in F	134	64
Camille Saint-Saëns	The Swan	140	69
	Air de Ballet	143	68
Franz Schubert	Symphony No. 5	138	70
Peter Ilyich Tchaikovsky	None but the Lonely Heart	144	70
	Dance of the Mirlitons	146	71
	Symphony No. 4	149	72
	Piano Concerto No. 1	150	72
	Symphony No. 6	150	73
	Barcarolle	152	74
Georg Philipp Telemann	Italian Air	156	76
Sebastián Yradier	La Paloma	158	77

Scherzino

Joachim Andersen
(1847–1909)

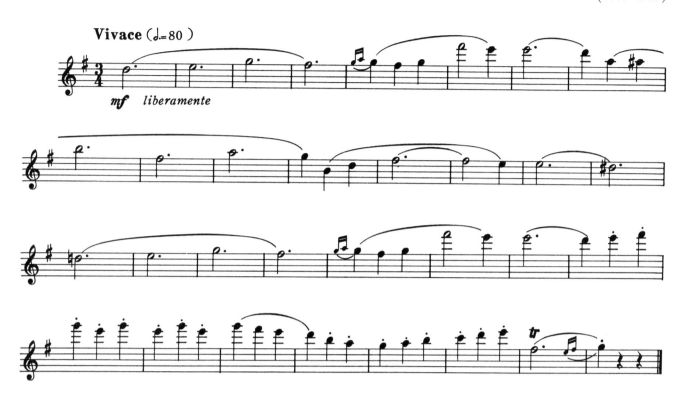

Minuet

Christmas

Johann Sebastian Bach
(1685–1750)

Gavotte

Johann Sebastian Bach
(1685–1750)

Sonata No. 2
(Second Movement)

Johann Sebastian Bach
(1685–1750)

Brandenburg Concerto No. 4
(Theme from First Movement)

Johann Sebastian Bach
(1685–1750)

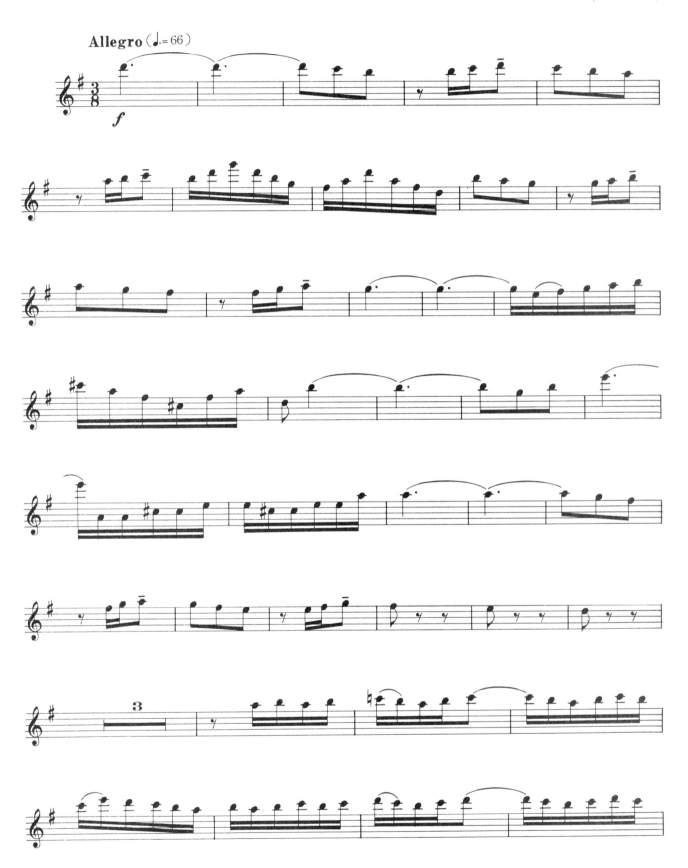

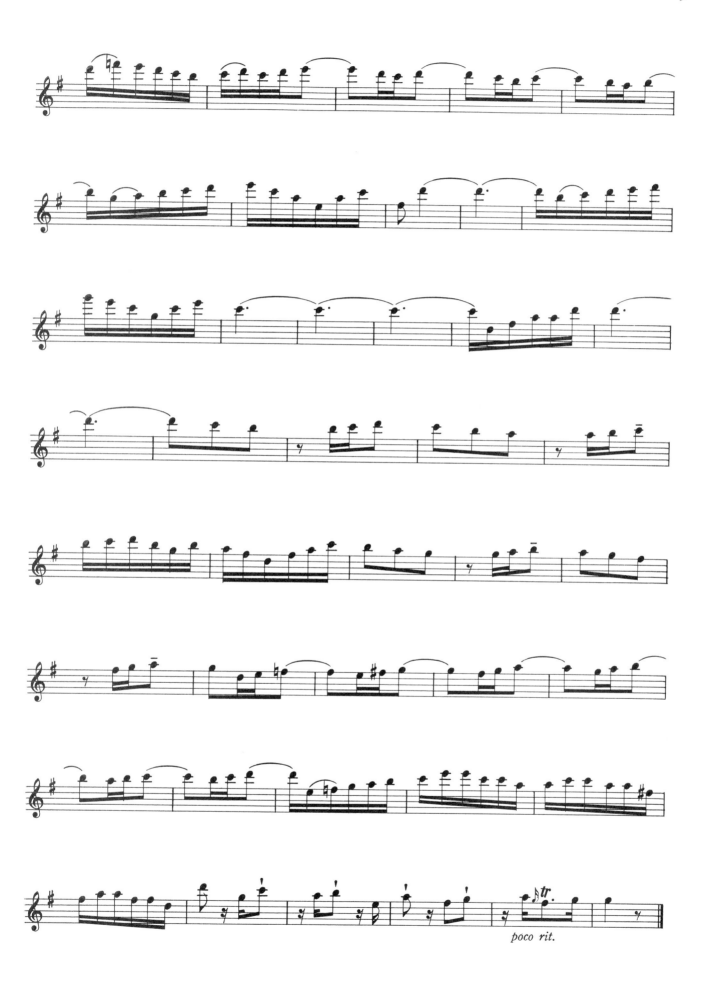

poco rit.

Brandenburg Concerto No. 5

(Theme from Third Movement)

Johann Sebastian Bach
(1685–1750)

poco rit.

Symphony No. 4
(Theme from Second Movement)

Ludwig van Beethoven
(1770–1827)

Symphony No. 7
(Theme from First Movement)

Ludwig van Beethoven
(1770–1827)

Symphony No. 9
(Theme from Third Movement)

Ludwig van Beethoven
(1770–1827)

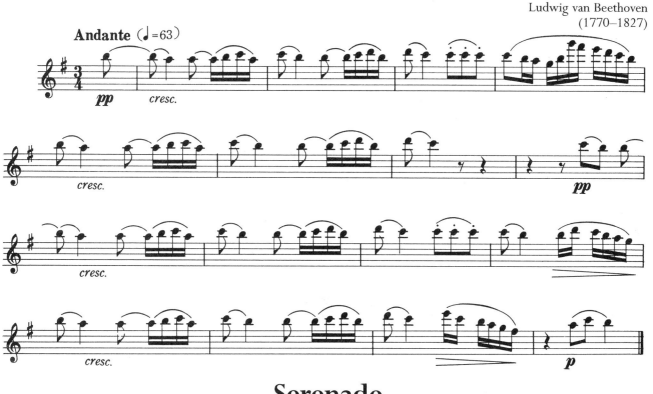

Serenade
(Excerpt)

Ludwig van Beethoven
(1770–1827)

Minuet in G

Ludwig van Beethoven
(1770–1827)

Symphonie Fantastique
(Theme from First Movement)

Hector Berlioz
(1803–1869)

Habañera

from *Carmen*

Georges Bizet
(1838–1875)

Allegretto quasi andantino

Concerto in D Major
(Theme from Rondeau)

Luigi Boccherini
(1743–1805)

Waltz

Johannes Brahms
(1833–1897)

Symphony No. 1

(Theme from Fourth Movement)

Johannes Brahms
(1833–1897)

Symphony No. 4

(Solo from Fourth Movement)

Johannes Brahms
(1833–1897)

Minute Waltz

Frédéric Chopin
(1810–1849)

Nocturne

Frédéric Chopin
(1810–1849)

Humoresque

Antonín Dvořák
(1841–1904)

Poco lento e grazioso

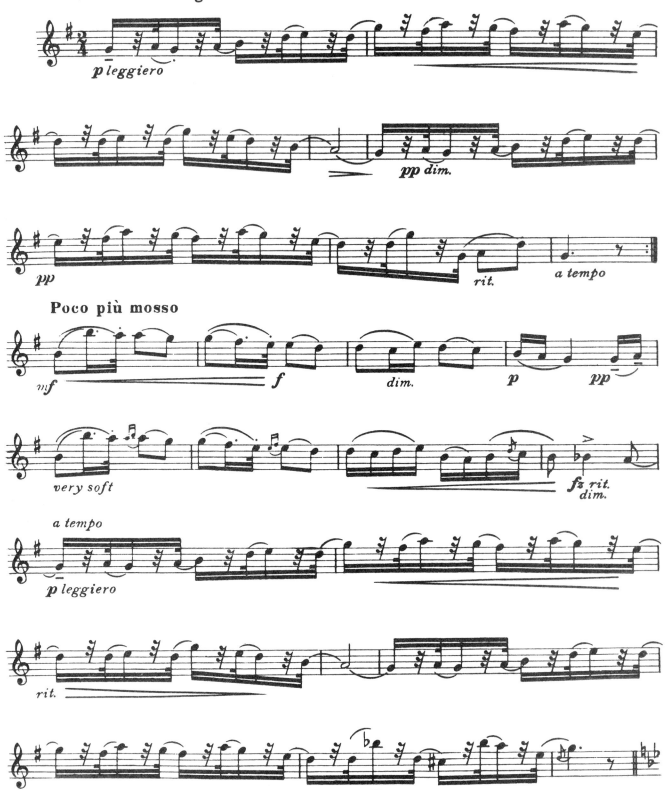

Un più mosso

Prelude to the Afternoon of a Faun

Claude Debussy
(1862–1918)

Rêverie

Claude Debussy
(1862–1918)

Ah! So Pure

from *Martha*

Friedrich von Flotow
(1812–1883)

Minuet and Dance of the Blessed Spirits

from *Orfeo ed Euridice*

Christoph Willibald von Gluck
(1714–1787)

Légende Pastorale
from *Scotch Scenes*

Benjamin Godard
(1849–1895)

Andante quasi adagio

Berceuse
from *Jocelyn*

Benjamin Godard
(1849–1895)

Sonata No. 5
(Fourth Movement)

George Frideric Handel
(1685–1759)

Sonata No. 2

George Frideric Handel
(1685–1759)

Serenade

Franz Joseph Haydn
(1732–1809)

Andante cantabile

Trio No. 4

Franz Joseph Haydn
(1732–1809)

Cradle Song

Miska Hauser
(1822–1887)

On Wings of Song

Felix Mendelssohn
(1809–1847)

Spring Song

Felix Mendelssohn
(1809–1847)

Scherzo
from *A Midsummer Night's Dream*

Felix Mendelssohn
(1809–1847)

Allegro vivace (♩.=88–92)

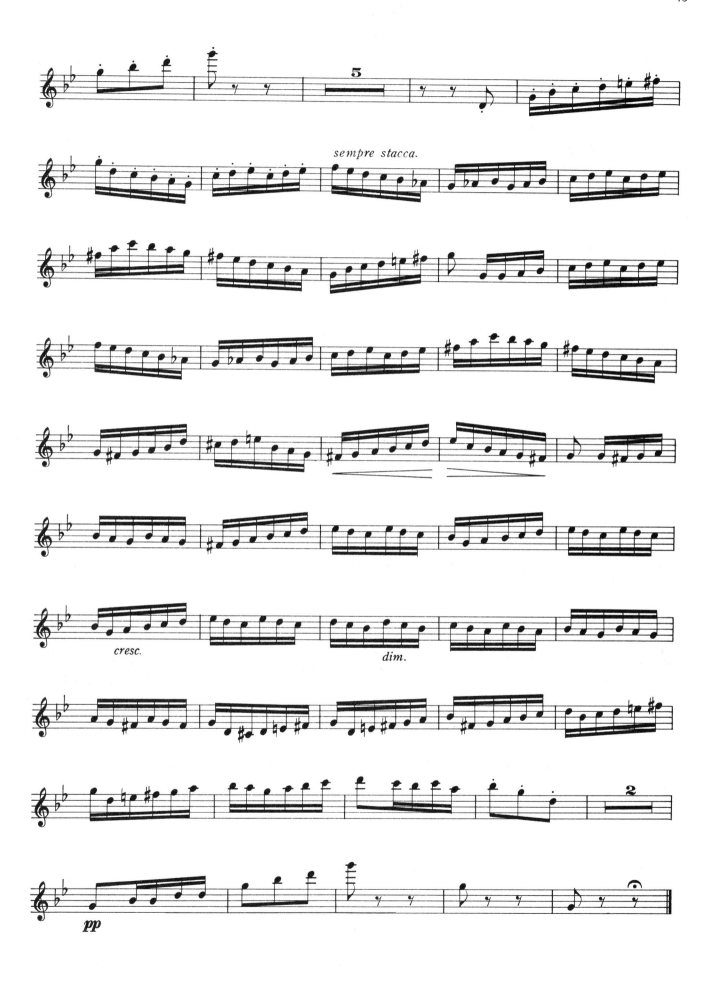

Quartet in D
(Second Movement)

Wolfgang Amadeus Mozart
(1756–1791)

Concerto No. 2

Wolfgang Amadeus Mozart
(1756–1791)

50

Cadenzas for Mozart Concerto No. 2

Joachim Andersen
(1847–1909)

Movement I

Movement II

Movement III

Barcarolle
from *Tales of Hoffman*

Jacques Offenbach
(1819–1880)

Allegretto

Andalouse

Émile Pessard
(1843–1917)

Arioso

Johann Joachim Quantz
(1697–1773)

Song of India

Nikolai Rimsky-Korsakov
(1844–1908)

Melody in F

Anton Rubinstein
(1829–1894)

Flight of the Bumblebee

Nikolai Rimsky-Korsakov
(1844–1908)

Scheherazade

Nikolai Rimsky-Korsakov
(1844–1908)

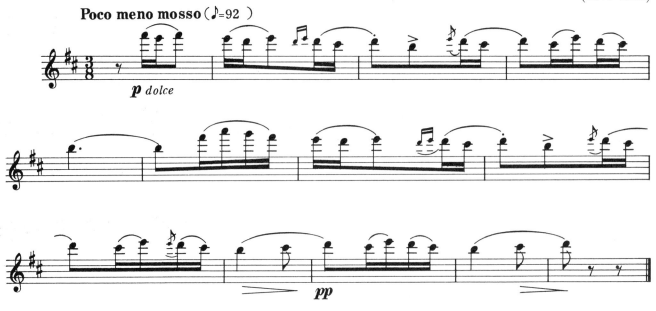

Air de Ballet

Camille Saint-Saëns
(1835–1921)

The Swan

from *Carnival of the Animals*

Camille Saint-Saëns
(1835–1921)

Symphony No. 5

Franz Schubert
(1797–1828)

Andante con moto ♪=84

None but the Lonely Heart

Peter Ilyich Tchaikovsky
(1840–1893)

Dance of the Mirlitons

from *The Nutcracker Suite*

Peter Ilyich Tchaikovsky
(1840–1893)

Symphony No. 4
(Theme from First Movement)

Peter Ilyich Tchaikovsky
(1840–1893)

Moderato con anima (♩.= **in movimendo di Valse**)

Piano Concerto No. 1
(Theme from Second Movement)

Peter Ilyich Tchaikovsky
(1840–1893)

Andantino sluplice

Symphony No. 6
(Theme from First Movement)

Peter Ilyich Tchaikovsky
(1840–1893)

Barcarolle

"June" from *The Seasons*

Peter Ilyich Tchaikovsky
(1840–1893)

Italian Air

from *Suite in A Minor*

Georg Philipp Telemann
(1681–1767)

La Paloma

Sebastián Yradier
(1809–1865)